Getting Ready for the Ball

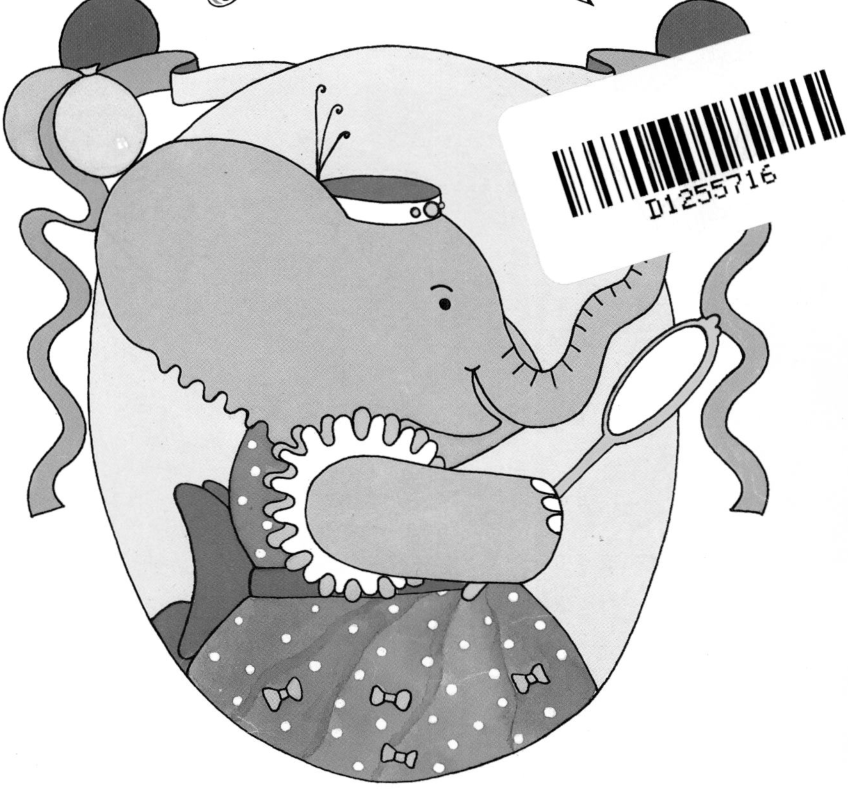

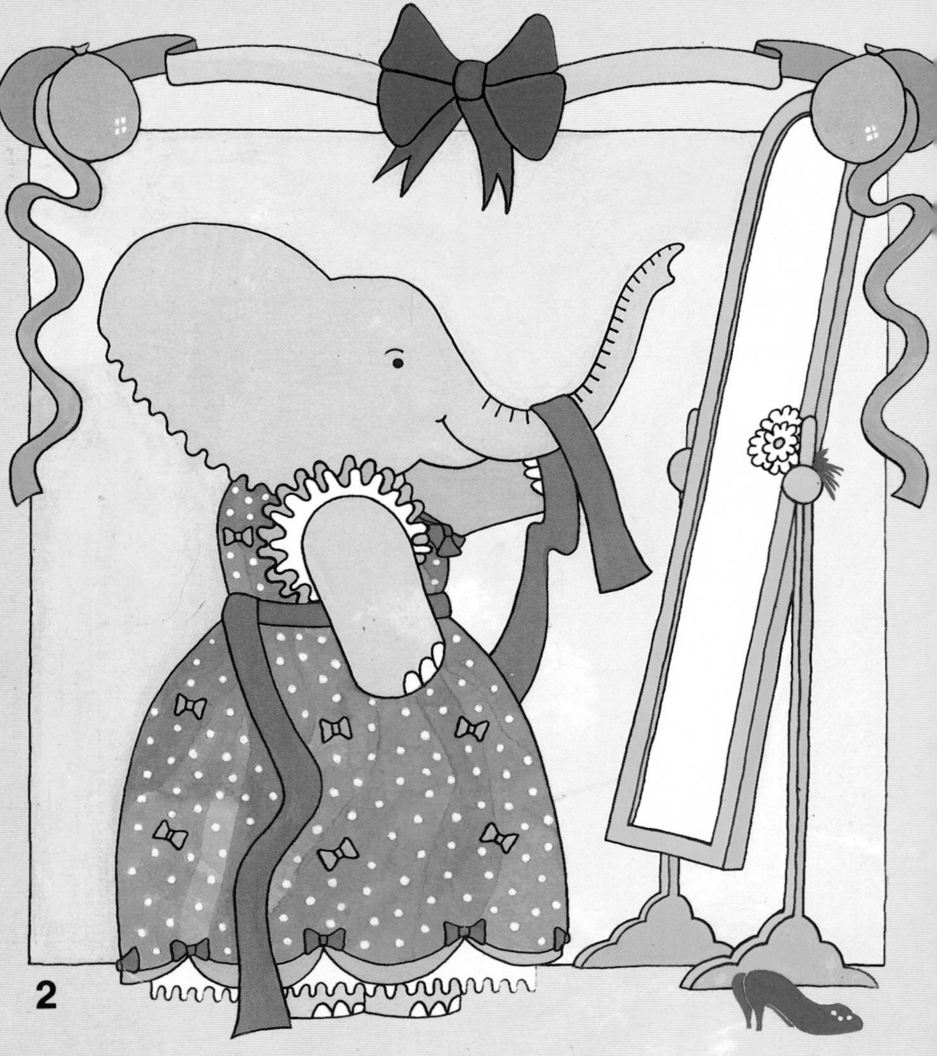

Jessie put on her dress,

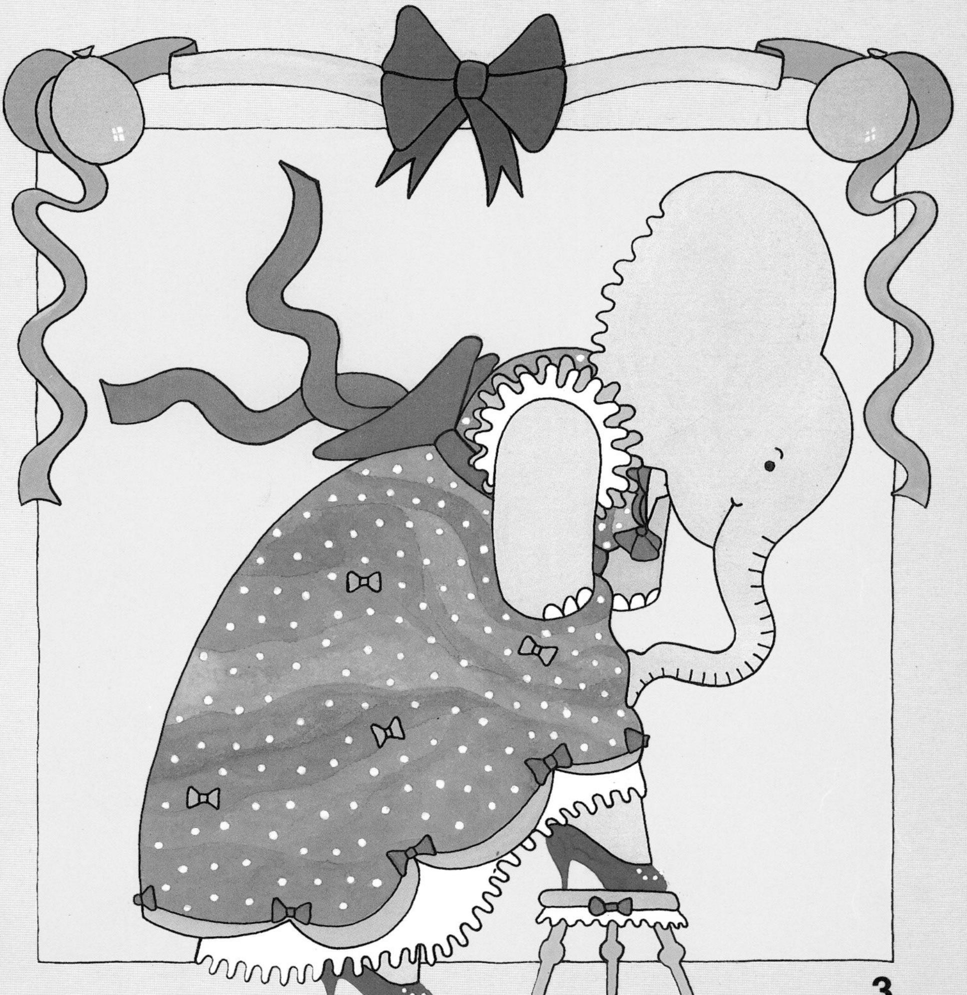

then her shoes,

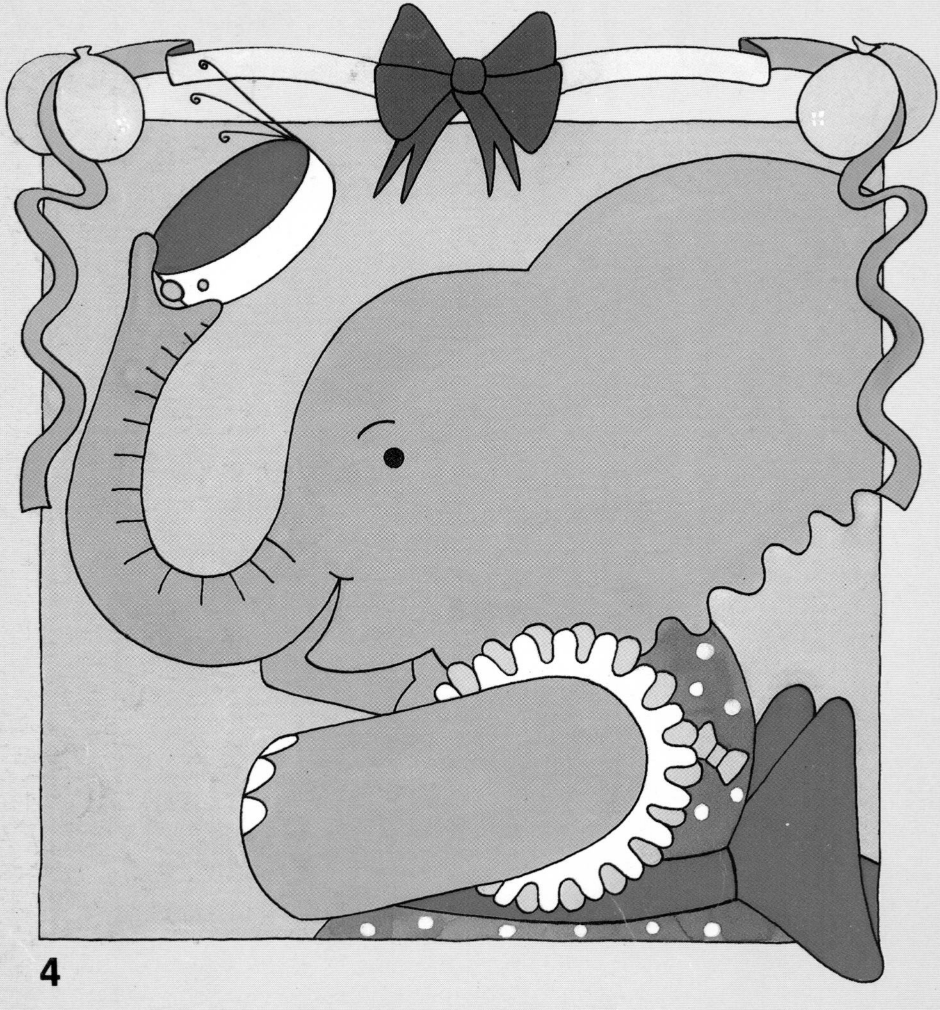

then her hat,

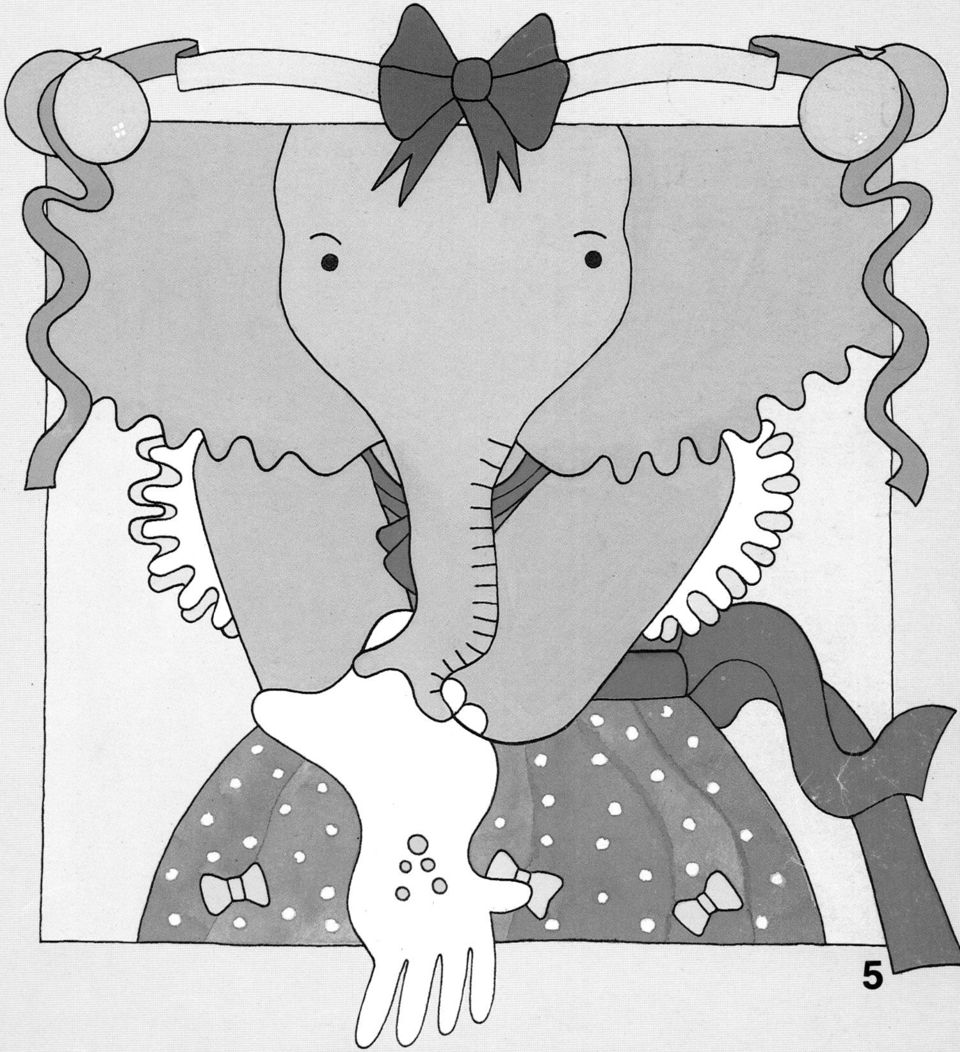

then her gloves,

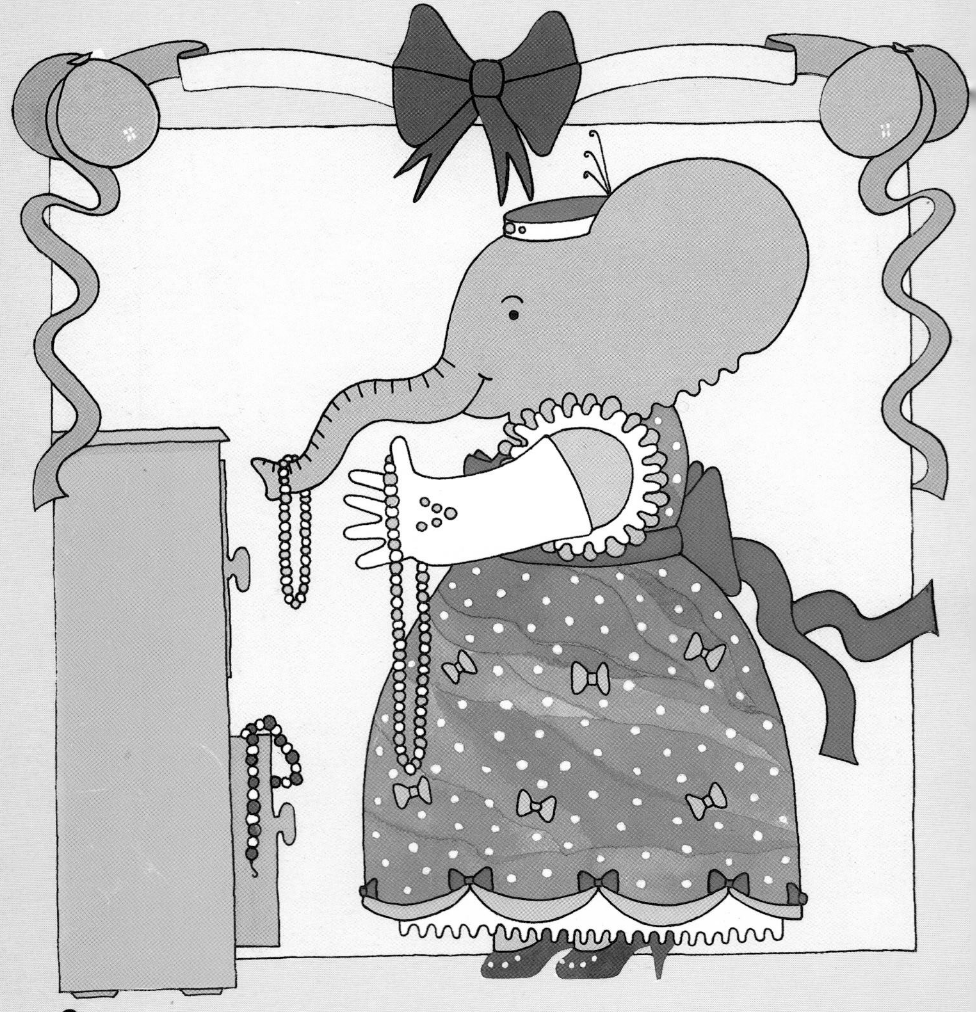

then her beads,

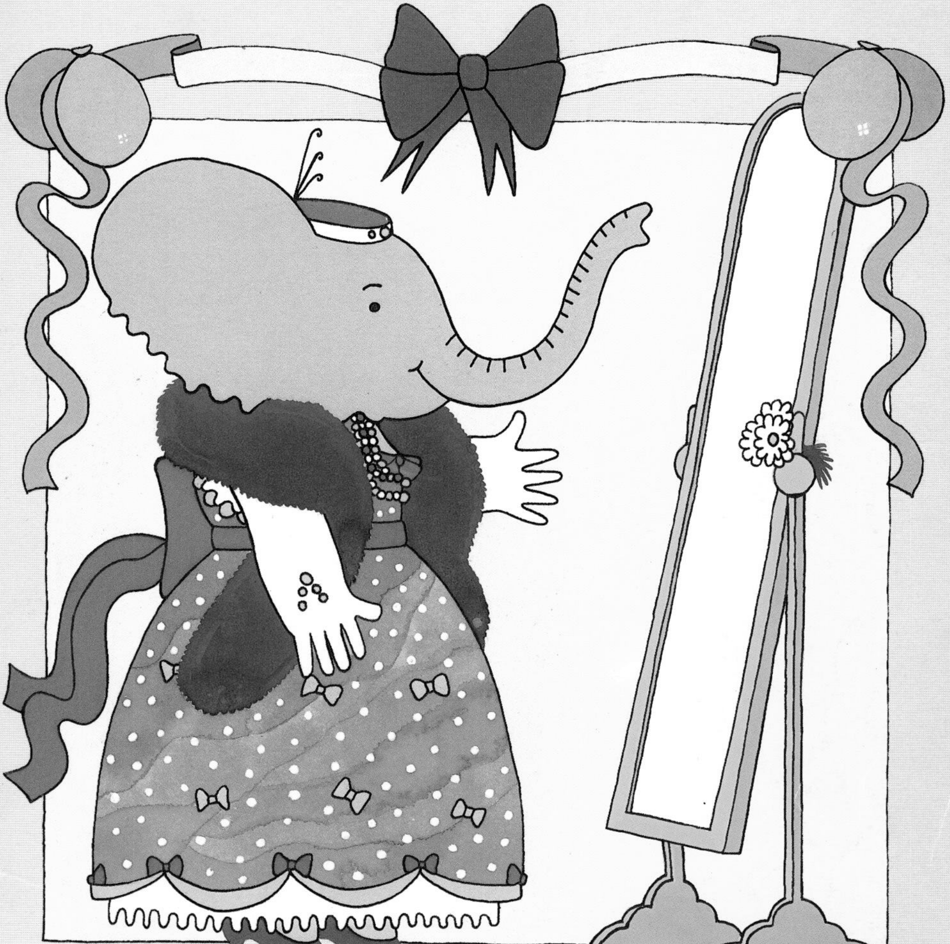

then her scarf.

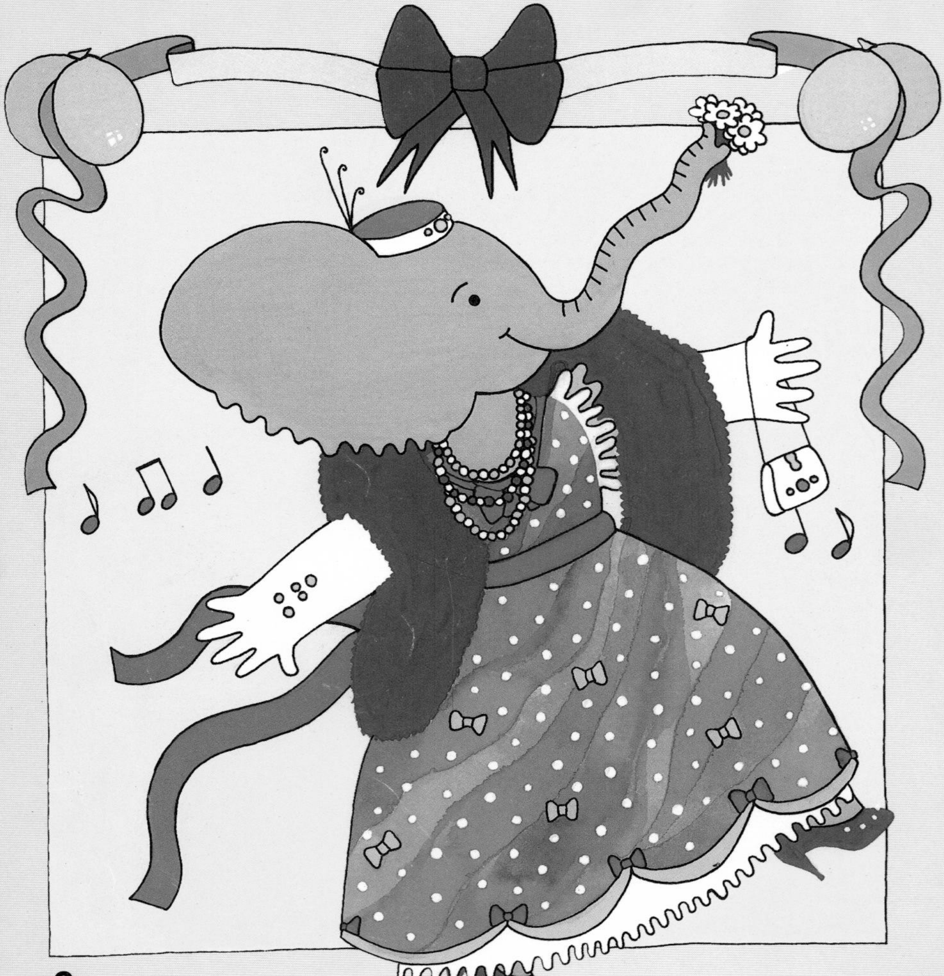

Then she was ready
for the ball.